FIRE TRUCKS

FIRE TRUCKS

Hope Irvin Marston

Illustrated with photographs

COBBLEHILL BOOKS   *Dutton*   *New York*

The photographs in this book are used by permission and through the courtesy of: Brion Bear, 38 (right); Bombadier, Inc., 27; Boston Whaler, Inc., 25; David Clark Company Inc., 19; W. S. Darley & Company, 13; Detex Corporation, 37; Bastian Freund, 31; Robert L. Irvin, 11, 12, 21, 40; Kenworth Truck Company, 15; Willian C. Locke, 39 (right); Arthur Marston, 29, 34, 38 (left), 39 (left); Mine Safety Appliances Company, 42; Okoboji Fire Department, 10; Oshkosh Truck Corporation, 23, 46; Phoenix USA, Inc. © 1995 All rights reserved, 41; Joe Pinto, 18, 24, 28, 32; Pierce Manufacturing Inc., 16; George C. Reichhardt, 20, 36; Brian Roderman, 47; *Watertown Daily Times*, 35; Watertown Fire Department, 6, 8, 9, 43; Richard P. Wersinger, 30, 33; Tim Winters, 44, 45; U.S. Forest Service, 26.

Library of Congress Cataloging-in-Publication Data
Marston, Hope Irvin.
Fire trucks / Hope Irvin Marston ; illustrated with photographs.—Rev. and updated ed.
p. cm.
Includes index.
Summary: Describes different kinds of firefighting equipment, such as pumper trucks, fireboats, and the SuperScooper, an airplane used to fight forest fires, as well as the work of people who put out fires.
ISBN 0-525-65231-0
1. Fire engines—Juvenile literature.   2. Fire extinction—Equipment and supplies—Juvenile literature. [1. Fire engines.   2. Fire fighters.] I. Title.
TH9372.M37 1996   628.9′25—dc20   95-47945 CIP AC

Published in the United States by Cobblehill Books,
an affiliate of Dutton Children's Books,
a division of Penguin Books USA Inc.
375 Hudson Street, New York, New York 10014

Designed by Jean Krulis
Printed in Hong Kong
First Edition 10 9 8 7 6 5 4 3 2

For Tara, Traci, and Travis

With special thanks to Battalion Chief Milton Sayre,
City of Watertown (NY) Fire Department

Red lights flash . . . sirens wail . . .
a charging fire truck roars down the street. It screeches to a halt in front of a burning building. Fire fighters leap to the ground and go to work.

The fire sizzles and crackles. A cloud of hot air and smoke pours out. It takes twenty-five minutes to bring the fire under control.

Welcome to the world of fire fighters. We are fortunate to have them. Every day they risk their lives to protect us from fires.

At the city fire station, fire fighters wash and polish their ladder truck. Others do their daily chores. Suddenly the public address system springs to life. Something is on fire. It is time to go. Sliding down the pole is the fastest way to get to the trucks.

The dispatcher strikes a tone which tells where the fire is located. Firemen pull on their rubber boots and grab their turnout coats and helmets. They leap into the fire truck and take off. The pumper and rescue truck zoom out right behind them.

Fire fighters use pumpers as attack vehicles. Pumpers carry water and powerful pumps for "getting the wet stuff on the red stuff." This pumper carries 1,000 gallons of water.

Firemen cool down a burning building before entering it to fight a fire. Large pumpers can squirt 3,000 gallons of water per minute on a fire. The force of the water is controlled by dials on the truck.

Firemen lay hose lines and connect them to the local water supply. If there is a hydrant nearby, soft suction hose that looks like canvas is used.

Sometimes there is no water available where a fire breaks out. Then a tanker carries water to the scene and refills the pumper or a portable tank. If water has to be brought from a river or pond, hard suction hose (those long "pipes" on the sides of a pumper or tanker) is used.

Pumpers carry ladders—for rescuing people, to enter or exit a building, to bridge an opening between buildings. A ladder can be used as a stretcher to remove an injured person from a burning upper story.

Pumpers also carry hand extinguishers and foam. Or axes and pike poles for breaking through windows or walls.

Small pumpers can whip through busy city streets or down country lanes faster than the larger ones. By the time they empty their tanks, the bigger pumpers or tankers arrive.

Ladder trucks carry wall ladders that are held in place by hand. Or extension ladders which come in sections, or roof ladders with hooks that fit over the peak of a roof.

Aerial ladders are attached to a turntable on the truck. They are built in sections that "telescope" inside each other. Some are more than 100 feet tall.

Aerial ladders help get fire fighters, equipment, and water to the upper stories of a building. Or to the roof. They can be used to rescue people.

Some aerial ladders have a platform or bucket at the top. This gives the fire fighters a place to stand and a better view of the fire. It's a dangerous place, though, because of smoke or freezing spray.

A Snorkel has a bucket platform that moves up and down like a giant elbow. Hose line runs up to the bucket. The bucket can reach out and over rooftops. And under, around, or between overhead wires. Support "arms" keep it from tipping.

Fire fighters sometimes carry out search and rescue missions. Some companies have trucks equipped with special gear like boats, ropes, and searchlights for finding and rescuing people.

Airports use a special kind of fire truck—a crash rescue vehicle (CRV). These heavy trucks have roof-mounted turret guns that shoot foam and chemicals onto the fire as they approach it.

If the plane's fuselage breaks in a crash, survival time is only a few seconds.

Port cities have fireboats to fight fires on ships and boats in the harbor, on islands and docks. They are like big tugboats with fire-fighting equipment. This includes scuba diving gear.

The world's largest fireboat is the *Fire Fighter*. It was built for the New York City Fire Department in 1938. It is still in use. It is docked at Staten Island.

Other places need a smaller boat that can zip around docks and harbors easily. The Boston Whaler is equipped with fire, rescue, and diving equipment.

Smoke jumpers parachute into forest fires to fight the flames. Their equipment and food are air-dropped to them.

Low-flying airplanes spray forest fires with chemicals and water. Helicopters lay hose lines up steep hillsides. They lower men and equipment into fire areas and rescue people from stricken areas.

The SuperScooper is an airplane built in Canada to fight wildfires in rough terrain. It's 65 feet long, 29 feet tall, with a wingspan of 94 feet. With twin turbo engines, it skims the water at high speed and scoops up water to fill its two 705-gallon tanks in just seconds. Computers control its four-door drop system.

The SuperScooper can make repeated drops for four hours without refueling.

Many fire fighters are volunteers. Others are paid professionals. All fire fighters spend hours and hours learning to put out fires fast. That includes handling hoses and checking equipment.

Fire fighters who must enter smoke-filled buildings wear air tanks connected to their face masks. This fire fighter is ready to join others on her team to make sure the fire is out.

The fireman opposite is manning the turret gun from atop his fire engine.

Sometimes firemen
have to chop a hole in
a building to get the
water inside . . .

. . . or drill a hole for the hose.

Fire fighters are trained to respond with speed, skill, and courage. Sometimes they form drill teams and have races as practice for fighting a fire. These races require teamwork and knowledge of the fire fighting equipment.

This ladder race results in spills for the team.

Smoke kills more fire fighters than flames, heat, or fire gases. That's why fire fighters wear air-packs.

Fire fighting is serious business. Many fire fighters are injured fighting fires. Saving a life is the fireman's first concern.

Fire fighters have a sense of humor. They take pride in
their profession and their equipment.

They show it with the pictures and names they use for
identification.

Years ago, fire engines were pulled by horses. Usually Dalmatian dogs ran alongside the horses to help clear the way and protect them from rats and robbers. Today, Dalmatian dogs often serve as mascots at fire stations.

Smokey models
her fire helmet.

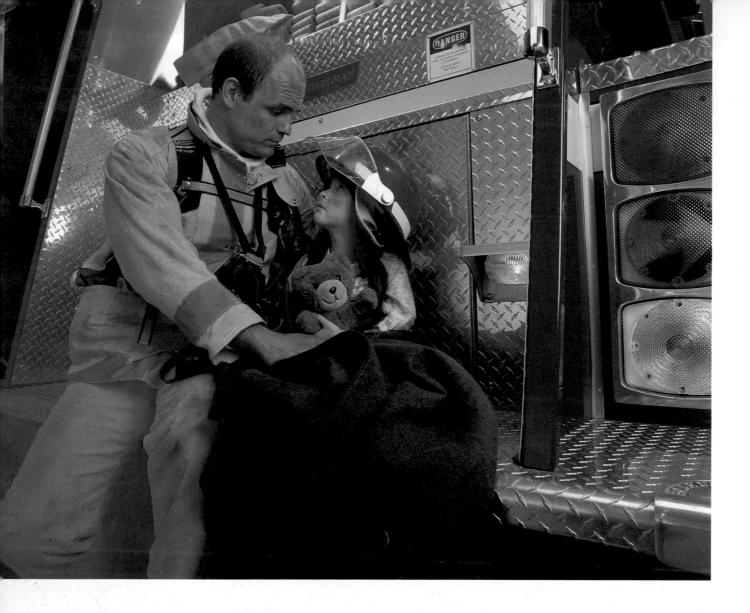

Fire fighters make every effort to rescue children. This little girl is comforted by the fireman who saved her.

Fire fighters like boys
and girls. If one comes to
your neighborhood,
welcome him and listen to
what he has to say.

Firemen will show you what to do when you are
trapped inside a burning building. If your clothing is on
fire, Stop, Drop, and Roll.

Stop and cover your eyes, nose, and mouth with your
hands. Drop to the floor. Roll over and over until the fire
is out.

Check a door for heat with the back of your hand before trying to open it. If the door is hot, find another way out.

If a room is smoky, keep your head up and crawl on your hands and knees to the nearest door or window.

What will fire trucks look like in the future? Not like
this old-fashioned truck.

Tomorrow's fire trucks may look like this. You don't see
ladders and hoses because they are enclosed.

INDEX